Wheeler's Vacation

Wheeler's

Vacation

by Daniel Schantz

Art by Ned O.

(s†u) STANDARD PUBLISHING
Cincinnati, Ohio   24-02912

Wheeler's Adventures

Library of Congress Cataloging in Publication Data

Schantz, Daniel.
  Wheeler's vacation / by Daniel Schantz ; art by
Ned O.
  p. cm. — (Wheeler's adventures ; 6)
  Summary: When the Wheelers drive from Mis-
souri to California on their vacation, Earnest bets
his brother Sonny that he won't have a good time
and then tries hard not to.
  ISBN 0-87403-452-3 (pbk.)
  [1. Brothers—Fiction. 2. Vacations—Fiction.] I.
Ostendorf, Edward, ill. II. Title. III. Series:
Schantz, Daniel. Wheeler's adventures ; 6.
PZ7.S3338Wl   1988
[Fic]—dc 19   88-9620

Cover illustration by Richard D. Wahl

to the Ron Self family,
fellow travelers on the road of life

Contents

1 • War

It came without warning. Sonny was just traipsing behind Earnest, headed up the driveway to their big blue house. In the distance horns were softly honking from a June wedding. A warm breeze carried the sweet aroma of strawberries from the garden. Sonny was kicking Earnest in the heels as he walked close behind him. Between kicks he teased him with smart remarks. Earnest just kept walking quietly toward the house.

Then Sonny made just one wisecrack too many. Earnest stopped walking. He turned and glared at Sonny. His face was purple and his lips tight and white. Without a word of warning, he squeezed his right hand into a fist, drew it back and thrust it straight to Sonny's face. Sonny tried to duck, but the fist landed square in the middle of his forehead with a terrible crunching sound. The next thing he knew, he was lying on his back in the gravel, unable to move a muscle.

Earnest gasped when he saw what he had done to his brother. He rubbed his sore right hand and looked around to see if anyone had seen him. Once more he gaped at his brother, lying mummy-like on the gravel driveway. Panic filled Earnest's eyes. He took a deep breath, sprinted to his bicycle, leaped on, and disappeared down the driveway.

Sonny opened his eyes, but something was blurring his vision. Slowly he reached up and felt his forehead. His hand closed over a large, hard swelling. "Ohhhhh," he moaned. "I'm dead. Ohhhhh, he killed me. Just look at me. Ohhhhh." He staggered to his feet, then fell back down.

The kitchen door cracked open. Mrs. Wheeler stuck her head out and looked around, as if she sensed something was wrong. When she spotted Sonny she heaved the door open, bounded down the steps and raced across the lawn to Sonny's side. She knelt over him just as he let out a long, animal-like moan.

"Sonny! What's wrong? Talk to me!" Gently she touched his swollen forehead. "How did this happen, Sonny? Say something!" She slapped his cheeks.

Sonny sat up with a groan. He leaned his head against his mother's shoulder. He was breathing in short jerks and sniffs.

"Earnest," he whispered. "Earnest hit me, for no reason at all."

Mrs. Wheeler frowned. "Earnest did this?"

Sonny nodded.

"I can't believe this! He could have killed you!" She swiveled her head, looking for Earnest.

In the house, Sonny shuffled to the kitchen table and dropped into a chair. His mother sat next to him, smearing the swollen forehead with salve.

"Can you see all right, Sonny? How many fingers am I holding up?"

Sonny mumbled, "Three."

"Can you hear me all right? Do you feel dizzy? Do you feel like throwing up? Who is President of the United States? What day is this? What is your middle name? Count to ten backwards."

Sonny mumbled the correct answers, then

added, "I'm okay, Mom. It just hurts like crazy, that's all." He took a deep breath and let it out slowly.

Satisfied, Mrs. Wheeler collapsed in her chair and sighed.

Ralph Wheeler's voice crackled on the kitchen intercom. "What's going on? Is something wrong?"

Mrs. Wheeler thumbed the button. "Tell you about it as soon as you come in for lunch. And it's almost ready."

When Mrs. Wheeler had filled all the plates with macaroni and cheese, the door opened and Mr. Wheeler trudged inside. He sniffed the air and wiped his greasy hands on a paper towel. "Smells good. I'm starved. Never seen so many people wanting cars fixed. Vacation, you know. Everybody wants his car in shape for traveling." Suddenly he stopped wiping his hands. His mouth fell open when he saw Sonny's head. "What the . . ."

"He's all right," Mrs. Wheeler explained.

"But what . . ."

"Earnest did it. We don't know why."

Mr. Wheeler looked around the room. "Where is Earnest?"

Mrs. Wheeler shrugged. "I dunno, but when he shows up, he's in big trouble."

Sonny grinned ever so slightly.

Lunch was almost over when the kitchen door creaked slowly open. There stood Earnest looking scared but determined. His black hair was wet from hard riding and his face was pale. His clean white shirt was stained with sweat.

The family glared at him. He shuffled in and sat at the table. He nibbled macaroni in silence while everyone watched. Mrs. Wheeler cleared her throat, as if she were about to deliver a speech.

Earnest waved her off. "Don't start it, Mom. I'm not even sorry about it."

"You're what? Ralph, you handle this. I'm afraid of what I might do to this child."

"I'm not a child, Mom, and I'm still not sorry."

Ralph Wheeler slowly stroked his mustache and studied his son for a while. "Son, we don't do this kind of thing in our family. When we have problems, we talk them out. I mean, this is how wars get started . . ."

"I don't want to hear your 'wars' lecture, Dad. I've heard it before." He shifted in his seat. "Sonny has been picking on me for a week and I just ran out of stuff to pick. I'm not made of stone."

Sonny rubbed his forehead and mumbled,

"Coulda fooled me." Mr. Wheeler looked Sonny straight in the eyes and Sonny flinched.

Earnest went on. "Sonny called me 'pretty boy' and 'Ernie.' I can take that, but I won't let him call me a 'fag,' just because I like to dress up and look nice."

Sonny swallowed so hard it could be heard. "I *said* I was sorry," he said, meekly.

"You didn't *mean* it," Earnest fired back.

"I did so! Don't tell me what I meant, mind-reader."

"And that's not all," Earnest added. "You broke my bike, and I told you to keep your clutzy body off of it."

"It was broken when I got on it."

"And then," Earnest continued, "as I was walking home, Sonny kept kicking me in the heels, like I was some tin can or something."

Mrs. Wheeler shook a finger at Earnest. "That's still no reason to punch your brother in the head. If you had hit him just right he could have gone blind or even died. Is that what you want?"

"Do I have to answer that?" Earnest said.

Mr. Wheeler waved his hands back and forth. "Wait a minute, wait a minute. What's going on here? Look at us. All of us. We've been fighting each other for two weeks like this. Joyce, we've been sharp with each other, too."

Joyce Wheeler nodded and started to clean up the table. "Maybe it's the weather? Or something, I don't know."

Ralph Wheeler pulled his wife to him with his strong right arm. He kissed her once, twice, three times. She blushed, and the boys giggled.

"I have a pretty good idea what's wrong," he said. "And I know what I'm gonna do about it."

"What?" Earnest asked with a trembling voice.

"You'll see. I'll tell you about it after supper. Meanwhile, I want you boys to shake hands, then come out to the garage and give me a hand."

Sonny looked at Earnest suspiciously, and Earnest returned the look. Sonny was first to extend his hand, and Earnest slapped it before shaking it firmly.

"I'm sorry," Earnest said. "I didn't mean to drop you." He grinned and added, "Just wanted to graze you a little."

Sonny grinned. "It would take more than *you* to put me outta business."

Earnest squinted up close at Sonny's welt on his forehead. "You know, you could get a nice part in a sci-fi movie."

2 • The Peace Plan

Ralph Wheeler stabbed the TV switch with his forefinger, and the picture vanished with a *blip*.

"Hey!" Sonny yelled, "that's my show."

His father ignored his protests and pulled a chair in front of the TV. He sat down facing the family.

Earnest groaned. "Oh, no, here it comes. The famous 'wars' lecture. I almost forgot about it."

Mr. Wheeler's face was somber. He cleared his throat twice and said, "I'm not going to put up with this fighting any more." Then his mustache curled up into a smile and his eyes began to twinkle. "We're going on a vacation! We are going to drive to California."

The room was still and quiet.

"Well," he added, "don't everybody cheer at once."

Earnest wrinkled his nose, and his voice took on a whining tone. "But Dad, we *can't*! I have the whole summer planned, right down to the minute. And I'll get kicked off Little League."

"Big deal," Sonny injected. "You're just the batboy."

Earnest went on. "And I bought a season pass to the swimming pool. And what about my paper route? And my yards? Who will mow my yards?"

Mrs. Wheeler spoke up. "Ralph, you're not serious?" In her eyes was a look of excitement mixed with fear. "I mean, it's a wonderful idea, but I've got a garden full of beans, strawberries, corn—"

"Give 'em to the neighbors."

"But what about the shop? You said yourself the cars are lined up for a mile."

"Exactly. Just why we need a vacation. Look, mine is not the only shop in town."

Mrs. Wheeler began to get a gleam in her eye. "Oh Ralph, it would be so much fun! We haven't had a vacation in five years. But California? It will cost us our entire savings."

Mr. Wheeler shook his head. "That's the beauty of it. Won't cost us much at all. See, the mechanics' association wants to send me to Los Angeles for some training meetings. They'll pay all our expense except personal things, you know, like camera film, treats . . ."

"Well, count me *out*," Earnest said. He got up to leave. "I'm not going and that's that. I'll stay at Howard's house if I have to."

"Whooooaaa," Mr. Wheeler stopped him. He pointed Earnest back to his chair. "I'm not asking, I'm *telling*." He paused to let his words sink in. The room was very quiet. He lowered his voice. "If we don't get a vacation, I'm afraid we might kill each other."

Earnest glanced at Sonny, and Sonny was rubbing his forehead as if to say, "You got that right."

"But it's so *boring*, traveling in a car," Earnest objected. "I hate it worse than anything."

Sonny jumped up, smiling. "Well, I don't think it sounds boring. I'm going to start packing. Will we get to see Grand Canyon?"

"Oh, sure, absolutely!"

"Big deal," Earnest growled. "A big gash in the

ground. World's biggest drainhole. I've seen sewers before."

Sonny turned to Earnest. "Better not let God hear you say that." He locked eyes with his brother. "The trouble with you, Earnest, is you don't know how to have fun. It's not the *trips* that are boring, it's *you* that's boring."

Mrs. Wheeler jumped into the argument. "Earnest, our forefathers sold their houses and lands and risked their lives for a chance to go west."

"Yeah? Well, they're all dead, you notice. They probably died of boredom." He folded his arms and frowned at the floor.

Mr. Wheeler put his hands on Earnest's shoulders and looked into his eyes. "Earnest, if you don't have more fun on this trip than you have had in your whole life, why I'll ... I'll eat my mustache." He tickled Earnest's nose with his mustache, but Earnest jerked away. He added, "You can be the navigator—read and maps and the travel guides, keep us on track."

"Oh, no!" Sonny said, throwing up his hands. "We'll be lost before we get out of the city limits."

"Sonny, you can be in charge of loading and unloading suitcases, since you are bigger."

Earnest smacked his forehead with his palm.

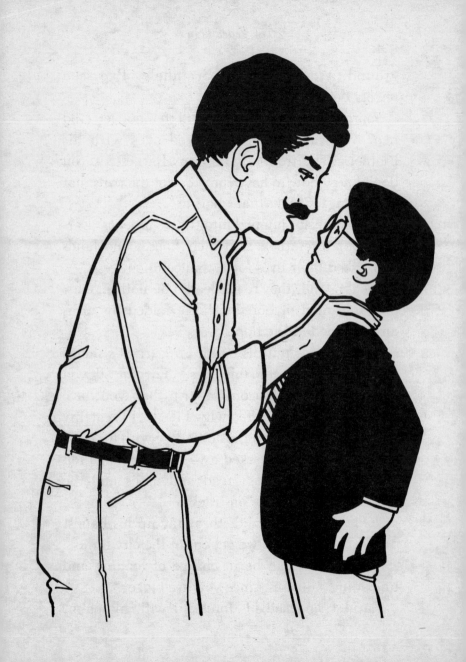

"That's just great! We'll be walking around naked by the time we get to Kansas. Sonny can't keep track of his own smell." He kicked the magazine across the carpet. "Now I *know* I'm not going." He stomped off to his room.

Mrs. Wheeler shook her head. "What are we gonna do, Ralph? I don't want to force the boy. I'm sure he won't be bored if he'll just give it a chance."

Sonny grinned. "Relax, Mom and Dad, I'll take care of it. He just needs a little *encouragement*."

Sonny strolled down the hall to Earnest's room. He found Earnest lying face down on his bed, kicking the mattress with his toes over and over and chewing on his pillow like a sick dog. Sonny sat down at the computer and began typing something. Earnest didn't even try to stop him.

Sonny tore the finished sheet from the printer and sat down on the bed beside his brother. "Okay, Earnest, here's the deal."

Earnest opened one eye. "What deal?"

The deal is, if I can't get you to have fun on this trip, I'll do your stupid paper route for a month. I'll give you the twenty dollars you spent on the swim pass, and I'll fix your stupid bike you said I broke but I didn't."

Earnest said nothing. Slowly he sat up and began to stroke his chin in deep thought. "And if I *do* have fun, what then? What's the sticker?"

Sonny pointed to the next paragraph and grinned. "And if you *do* have fun"—his eyes were gleaming—"then you have to help me with my homework again like last year."

Earnest stiffened and shook his head. "No way! I told you I was never gonna get stuck doing that again, and I meant it."

"Fine. Then all you have to do is be bored. It should be a snap."

Earnest grabbed the contract and read it again. "But how will you know if I'm having fun? I mean I'm not gonna *tell* you, for pity's sake. How dumb do you think I am?"

Sonny laughed. "That's the easy part, Earnest. You always say the same thing when you are really enjoying yourself."

"I do? What?"

"You always say, 'Yo!' You get big eyes and you say, 'Yo!' every time."

Earnest puckered his face. "I do? Really? Oh, what a goober."

"You said it. So if I can get you to say 'Yo' just three times on this trip, I win. It's simple."

Earnest studied the contract a long time in silence. Then he grabbed a pencil and scribbled something else in between two paragraphs.

What are you doing?" Sonny asked.

Earnest jumped up and headed for the kitchen. "Follow me." He shoved the contract in his father's face. "Here, sign this, Dad."

"Huh? What's this?" Mr. Wheeler looked at the contract.

"Sonny and I have a deal, and you're part of it. You said if I didn't have more fun on this trip than I've ever had in my life, then you would eat your mustache."

"But I . . ." He started to object, but then he saw that special look in Earnest's eyes. With a sigh he reached for a pen and scrawled his name at the bottom of the paper. Sonny added his name, and Earnest finished the ceremony by adding his initials.

Then Earnest smiled ear to ear. His eyes glowed like gemstones. He rolled up the contract, tapped it twice on Sonny's head and said, "Yo!"

At bedtime, Sonny and Earnest were sprawled out on the living room floor. The TV was on, but both of them were reading. Sonny was reading the travel guidebooks.

"Earnest, there are hundreds of things to see on this trip. Look at this list: gold mines, ghost towns, wax museums . . ."

"Boring," Earnest mumbled without looking up from his computer book.

"And there are Indian ruins and hot springs, rodeos, aquariums, museums. Look at all the museums."

Earnest yawned. "If you've seen one museum, you've seen 'em all."

Sonny went on. "Here is a whole list of theme parks, fish hatcheries, dinosaur parks . . ."

Earnest scowled at Sonny. "Do you mind? I'm trying to read."

Sonny paid no attention. He went on reading eagerly. "And libraries—look at all the libraries listed here."

"Huh?" Earnest put down his books at last.

"I said libraries. The space science library, the John Steinbeck Library, the Eisenhower Library, state libraries . . ."

Earnest raised an eyebrow. "Really?"

Sonny stared blankly at Earnest. "I suppose you thought the Mulberry Library is one of a kind in the world?" Sonny went on reading. "There's a couple 'o mints, too."

"Mints?"

"You know, places where they make money. There's one in Denver and another one in San Francisco. The one in San Fran has gold bars on display and a grizzly bear made of solid gold."

Earnest sat up. "That's interesting. Wonder if they give free samples."

"We might even get to go through Silicon Valley. Computer capital of the world," Sonny added. He staggered to his feat and headed for his room. "I'm gonna get some shut-eye. See ya." He shuffled away.

Earnest reached for the travel book and began to explore it. "Hmmm," he said to himself. "I never knew there were so many interesting things in the west. This might be harder than I thought."

3 • Good-byes

Late Sunday night the Wheelers finished packing. A mountain of luggage filled the center of the dining room. Off in one corner Earnest was sprawled out on the floor on a pile of open road maps. "Looks like we take the interstate most of the way," he said.

When Cherry, the neighbor girl, came to say good-bye, she stood quietly in the doorway and watched the family pack. She was wearing an old, wrinkled dress and faded tennis shoes. She was not smiling like everyone else.

Mrs. Wheeler was the only one who noticed. She stooped beside Cherry and put her arm around her.

"What's wrong, Hon?"

Cherry's lip quivered, and she spoke in a whisper. "I wish I was going on a trip." She took a deep breath and added, "I never go anywhere." Her eyes had a faraway look in them.

Mrs. Wheeler hugged her tightly. "I'm sorry, Cherish. I wish we could take you with us."

"No, I didn't mean that. I wasn't hinting. I guess I'm just going to miss everybody so much . . ." Her eyes began to fill with tears. She spun around and stumbled toward the kitchen door. "Good-bye, everybody," she tried to say, but just a squeak came out.

Only Earnest slept that night. Sonny was sitting up in bed, holding his alarm clock right in his lap when it went off Monday at five a.m. The house soon buzzed with activity. In a few minutes the car was loaded with luggage and people. Seat belts snapped in place. Mr. Wheeler twisted the ignition key and said, "Los Angeles, here we come. And may the good Lord take care of us."

The big white car groaned from all the unusual weight. It rocked and dipped like a boat as it

headed out the bumpy drive and down the narrow street. The sky was just beginning to glow with light.

Mrs. Wheeler looked back at the house. "Good-bye, old house," she said, wistfully.

Sonny looked back too. "Good-bye, old Studebaker. Good-bye bicycle."

Earnest turned and watched the house growing smaller. "Good-bye office, good-bye computer . . . good-bye civilization."

"Good-bye Long Branch Lake, front yard, trees, trash cans," Sonny added.

Mr. Wheeler joined in. "Good-bye cars and kerosene, oil and grease—and good riddance."

A funny look came over Sonny. "Good-bye bathroom," he said, then added, "Dad, I've got to go to the bathroom."

"What?!" Mr. Wheeler almost drove off the road.

"I gotta go to the bathroom!"

"Well you can just forget it. I'm not stopping for a long time."

"Okay, but you'll be sorry," Sonny said under his breath.

Everyone was asleep when Mr. Wheeler turned the car onto the freeway. For an hour he hummed to himself happily as the car whined through the morning stillness.

Sonny was first to wake up when the traffic got heavier. He craned his neck and looked around. "Where are we, Dad?"

"Coming into Kansas City."

Sonny spotted the Royals' baseball stadium off to his left. Thousands of brilliant red seats shone in the morning sun, and a huge golden crown towered above them, symbol of royalty.

Sonny shook Earnest. "Look, Earnest! The Royals' stadium!"

Earnest opened one eye, then closed it. He mumbled, "I'm a Cardinals fan myself."

Sonny sneered. "I think this is gonna be harder than I thought. I was sure that would get a 'Yo!' out of him."

The traffic grew heavier as they wove through the middle of Kansas City. Mrs. Wheeler woke, then Earnest finally sat up and stretched.

"Dad, I gotta get to a rest room real bad," Sonny reminded his father, but his father was busy watching traffic.

Suddenly the four lanes of traffic narrowed to two lanes, then came to a halt near a cloverleaf of bridges and exits.

"Oh, great!" Mr. Wheeler said. "Just great. Look at that!" A construction worker was holding up a sign that said, "Construction delay of five minutes." Mr. Wheeler shut off the engine and slapped the steering wheel in disgust.

"Relax," Mrs. Wheeler said. "We're in no hurry, Ralph. We're on vacation, remember?"

All at once the back door flew open and Sonny leaped out. He sprinted through the stalled cars and leaped over the metal railing.

"What the . . ." Mr. Wheeler said with a loud voice. "What does he think he's doing?"

"Get back here, Sonny!" Mrs. Wheeler shouted.

Earnest sat up. His mouth dropped open when he saw Sonny scrambling up an embankment and disappearing behind a bridge piling. "Yo!" he said. "Where's he goin'?"

In a few moments Sonny appeared again, slid down the bank, danced through the cars and leaped into his seat just as the traffic started moving again.

Mr. Wheeler glared at him as he put the car in gear. "Don't you ever pull a stunt like that again, Sonny, or I'll—"

"But Dad, I *told* you an hour ago I had to go."

Mrs. Wheeler took Sonny's side. "Ralph, he's

right. You know Sonny has always had a problem
that way."

The family was quiet for the next few minutes.
Earnest opened a Kansas map and began looking
it over.

Mrs. Wheeler turned around and smiled at
Sonny. "Sonny, your brother said 'Yo!' back there."

"He did? When?"

Earnest stiffened. "You can't prove it, Sonny
boy, 'cause you didn't hear it."

"But—"

"No buts about it. You have to catch me saying
it, or it doesn't count."

Sonny sat back in his seat and crossed his arms
with a grumpy look.

Earnest thumbed through the travel guidebook,
but not really reading it. "We'll soon be in Kansas," he said. "Anything important ever happen in
Kansas?"

Mr. Wheeler scratched his head. "A lot of fa-
mous cowboys used to live here—Jesse James,
Wyatt Earp . . . oh, and Matt Dillon, and Buffalo
Bill."

"Just think," Mrs. Wheeler chimed in. "Here we
are driving along at sixty miles an hour in perfect
comfort. Our forefathers rode this route in cov-

ered wagons and stagecoaches. It must have been pretty rough."

"I'll bet they had more fun," Sonny said. "I think it would be neat to bounce along in an old wagon, with Indians chasing you and rattlesnakes nipping at your toes."

Earnest rolled his eyes. "*You* would."

Mr. Wheeler pointed to his left. "The Little House on the Prairie is down south about a hundred miles. Over that way is Wichita, where they make airplanes. The first helicopter was made in Kansas."

Earnest yawned and dropped back in his seat.

Sonny spoke up. "Hey, isn't Kansas where Dorothy lived, in *The Wizard of Oz*?"

"That's right," Mrs. Wheeler replied. "Kansas has a lot of tornadoes, like the one that carried her away from home."

Earnest leaned his head against the window and closed his eyes. "Wow," he mumbled. "So much excitement it makes me sleepy to think about it."

4 • Close Call

Welcome to Kansas, the Sunflower State, said the yellow sign.

"All right!" Sonny yelled. "We're in another state. Now we're cookin'."

Earnest curled his lip. "Big deal. Do you know how *long* this state is? We'll be in Kansas for *years.*"

Mrs. Wheeler pulled a couple of envelopes from her purse and handed them to the boys. "Here, maybe this will sweeten the trip a little, Earnest."

The boys ripped open their envelopes.

"Hey, a fifty-dollar bill!"

"I got one too! Thanks, Mom!"

"It's spending money," she explained. "But I warn you, it will go very fast, so—"

Sonny pointed out the window. "Oh, look at that, look at that! Sunflowers! Look at 'em. Must be a million of 'em."

As far as the eye could see stretched lazy fields of big yellow sunflowers, their heavy heads bowed in the hot sun. Birds and butterflies skipped from head to head like ballet dancers.

"Oh, yippee," Earnest said with mock excitement. "Who in the world would plant a whole field of sunflowers, anyway?"

"Cherry would," Mrs. Wheeler said. "I want you boys to send some postcards to Cherry. Poor little lady, she cried when we left. I feel so sorry for her sometimes."

"They grow sunflowers for the oil," Mr. Wheeler added. "The kind you boys use to make your popcorn."

The afternoon dragged along. Earnest pulled his briefcase from the back window and snapped it open. It was neatly packed with books, magazines, and snack items. He popped a cheese curl in his mouth and thumbed through the auto club guidebook. Sonny put on his headphones and listed to music as he watched the fields roll by.

At last Mr. Wheeler pulled off the interstate to get gasoline. Earnest strolled into the station to use the rest room. Sonny leaped out and bounded next door to a convenience store. The Kansas wind pushed him along as he leaped and skipped to the door. Soon he came out with a super-sized soft drink in his hand. He slurped his way back to the car. He was almost across the grass when he spotted a small garter snake sunning itself just inches from his foot. He captured the twisting, wriggling creature in his right hand and studied it closely before popping it into his shirt pocket.

"No wonder you always need a rest room," his father said, when he saw the giant soft drink.

Back on the road again, Sonny finished his drink and Earnest went back to sleep. Sonny unbuttoned his shirt pocket and played with the snake until he too began to tire from the long and weary road. He fell asleep, and the snake slid out of his limp hand and dropped to the floor. It disappeared under the seat.

When the boys awoke it was late in the afternoon. Mrs. Wheeler was still asleep. Earnest checked his map. "We just passed Russell. We're only halfway across this miserable state." He slumped back in his seat and sighed.

Sonny reached for his empty soft drink cup. With a pencil he began punching holes in the rim of it. Then he fished a skein of orange yarn from his mother's sewing bag and tied it in the holes.

"What are you up to?" Earnest asked, but Sonny just smiled.

"Watch this." He shoved the cup out the side window and let out some yarn. The cup floated behind the car like a little kite.

"Let some more line out," Earnest urged. More of the orange string slid through Sonny's fingers. Now the cup was floating two car lengths behind and Earnest began to chuckle.

"What are you boys up too?" Mr. Wheeler called over his shoulder.

"Just playing with string," Sonny replied calmly. More line slid through his fingers. Now the cup was almost a hundred feet behind them, bobbing and dipping like a drunken bird.

"Uh-oh," whispered Sonny. "Here comes a car."

"That's okay," Earnest replied. "The cup is higher than the car. Just leave it there."

The car drew closer and closer until the cup was floating right above it.

"Sonny!" Earnest screamed in a whisper. "*It's a highway patrolman! Let it go, let it go!*"

"I can't! This is Mom's yarn, she'll kill me!"

"Not if the police shoot you first. Let it go!"

Sonny held fast. "I don't think he sees it." Just then the patrolman's lights burst into life, and his car swung to the other lane.

"We're *dead!*" Earnest said. "We're going to spend our vacation in jail thanks to you, Sonny."

The patrolman pulled alongside. "Whoa!" Mr. Wheeler said, when he saw the flashing lights. "We've got company." He checked his speed and slowed to pull over, but the patrol car only whizzed on by.

"Whew," Mr. Wheeler said. "I thought he was going to stop me, but I guess he's on his way to check out an accident."

Sonny collapsed in his seat, and Earnest collapsed on top of him. "That was *close*," Earnest whispered.

Sonny wound in the yarn and slipped it into his mother's sewing bag just before she woke up. She stretched twice, then said, "Ralph, don't you think it's getting warm in here?"

Mr. Wheeler rolled up the windows and flipped on the air conditioner.

Ten seconds later, Mrs. Wheeler let out an ear-shattering scream. "Yiiiii!" She flattened back in her seat.

"Joyce! What's wrong? What is it?"

She pointed to the air conditioning vent. Sticking out of it was the small green head of Sonny's snake. Its beady eyes were staring at Mrs. Wheeler, and its tongue snapped in and out like a little red flag.

Earnest jumped up and saw the snake protruding from the vent. "YO!" he shouted.

The car skidded to a stop. Mrs. Wheeler leaped out and began running down the road. Mr. Wheeler gently coaxed the little snake out of the vent and flung it into the ditch. Then he turned around and glared at Sonny and Earnest. "I don't know where the snake came from, but I don't think it was put there at the factory."

Both boys blinked but said nothing.

Mr. Wheeler coaxed his wife back into the car, but she sat close to the door and kept her eye on the air conditioner vents.

"What if there's a whole nest of snakes in there?" Earnest teased.

"Yeah," Mr. Wheeler added, "and that one was just the baby."

Sonny kept quiet. Mrs. Wheeler turned and stared at the boys. "When I find out which one of you brought that animal into this car . . ."

The boys looked at each other and smiled. Then Sonny whispered in his brother's ear, "You *said* it. You said 'Yo.'" I heard you! That's *one*. Two to go."

A look of horror came over Earnest. Then it changed to a look of daring. "You'll never get me again," he vowed. *"Never."*

He sat back in his seat and pulled a small sack of pretzels out of his briefcase. For a while he munched on the salty snacks as he studied the passing scenery with a scornful look on his face.

"Why did God invent Kansas, anyhow? Was He

running out of things to invent?" He waved his arm toward the window. "Just look at it. Miles and miles of nothing. Fields and fields of dirt and wheat."

Mr. Wheeler gave him a serious look.

Earnest went on griping. "At least they could have built some big cities or lakes or something to break it up. I'd settle for a big boulder here and there."

Again Mr. Wheeler looked back at his son. This time his face was red and his lips were taut, but Earnest didn't notice the warning. He went right on complaining.

"Does the wind ever quit around here? This would be a good place to send prisoners for punishment," he mumbled through a mouthful of pretzels. "Better yet, we could just give Kansas to the Russians as a practical joke. What a worthless piece of nothing."

Mr. Wheeler braked the car hard and pulled off the road.

Sonny jumped up. "What's wrong?"

Mr. Wheeler did not reply. He got out of the car and opened the back door. By the wrist he grabbed Earnest and pulled him out of the car. Then he turned and tromped down the bank and out into a plowed field. Earnest staggered along behind him, trying to keep up. His left hand was locked in his father's hand and his right hand clung to a pretzel.

Sonny and his mother watched this action with concern. "What's he doin' with Earnest?" Sonny asked.

Mrs. Wheeler just shrugged. "I haven't the foggiest idea. Maybe he's gonna bury him for complaining so much."

At last Mr. Wheeler stopped and let go of Earnest. He stooped down at the edge of the freshly-turned sod and plunged Earnest's hand into the soft soil. Earnest looked puzzled, and then he lifted up a handful of the rich loam and sniffed it.

"Do you know what this is?" his father asked.

"Dirt, I'll bet."

"Not dirt. *Topsoil*. Precious, valuable topsoil." He scooped up a handful himself. "Ten inches of pure gold. Nations only last as long as their topsoil, did you know that?"

Earnest clamped his last pretzel between his lips and shook his head.

Mr. Wheeler added, "Every farmer in Kansas feeds an average of a hundred other people besides him and his family. People all over the world."

His face was no longer red. He reached up and tugged at the pretzel in Earnest's mouth and popped it into his own mouth. He offered Earnest a hand, and together they started back to the car. "So, Earnest, what I'm trying to say is, 'Don't bite the hand that feeds you.'" He crunched the pretzel in his big teeth and made sounds of enjoyment.

5 • Rocky Mountain High

"*This* is Colorado?" Mrs. Wheeler asked. "It's flatter than Kansas."

"We don't get to the mountains till Denver," Earnest called from the back seat. He and Sonny were playing an electronic game. Strange lights and noises floated up from the back seat.

Mr. Wheeler stopped at a truck stop in Limon, and the family gorged on homemade cinnamon rolls and juice. The boys filled their pockets with travel brochures from the rack, then sprinted back to the car.

"I'll see the mountains before you do," Sonny boasted.

"Oh?" Earnest replied. Calmly he opened his briefcase and pulled out a pair of binoculars. "We'll just see about that."

Sonny bounced on the edge of his seat, chewing his fingernails. "I've never seen real mountains," he said. "Wonder what they are like?"

"They're like anthills, only bigger," Earnest said, glancing at his guidebook. "Mt. Evans is over 14,000 feet high."

Sonny rolled his eyes. "That's almost three miles high. What if we fall off?"

Earnest punched some numbers on his calculator. "If you fall off, you would be dead in exactly a hundred and forty-five seconds, so you wouldn't have a lot of time to worry."

An hour passed. Suddenly Sonny stopped fidgeting and began to lock eyes with the horizon. "I see 'em! I see 'em! Mountains, dead ahead! Rock ho!"

Earnest sat up straight. "Where? Those aren't mountains, those are just clouds . . . aren't they? They couldn't be moun—" He twisted the focus of his binoculars. "He's right, the goober is right! Mountains! And they've got white icing on them."

"That's snow," Mr. Wheeler said. His voice was electric.

"Snow? In June?"

"Sure. It's cold up at 14,000 feet, you know?"

As the Wheelers rolled into Denver, a steady line of jumbo jets rumbled overhead and settled softly to the city in front of them. Sonny snapped several pictures of the wide city with the frosted mountains in the background.

"Look!" Sonny cried out. "The runway! The airport runway goes right over the highway. We go right under the big jets."

"Oh, creepy," Earnest replied. "We'll be crushed." He ducked as the car passed under the runway.

"You said 'Yo,'" Sonny said.

"I did not, I said 'Oh.'"

"Just checking."

The ride through Denver gave them a half hour of relief from the boring flatlands of Kansas and eastern Colorado. Then they watched the city grow smaller through the back window as the car headed up into the Rocky Mountains.

"Uh-oh," Mr. Wheeler mumbled. "Something's wrong with the car. We're barely moving and I have the pedal to the floor."

Earnest pointed at a sign. "There's what's wrong. We're at six thousand feet and climbing up ten degrees."

"You know, I believe you are right, Earnest. These mountains must be huge."

The afternoon was a blur of fun for everyone. The car groaned up one mountain, then screamed down the other side. All around, the rocky forms of snow-splashed mountains towered like friendly monsters. The air was cool and clean, and large birds sailed nearby in it.

At Idaho Springs they stopped to see the Argo Goldmill, and the boys panned for gold in a frigid mountain stream.

"I didn't find any gold," Earnest complained. "I knew I wouldn't."

At the little village of Georgetown they stopped and fished for trout in a crystal mountain lake. Sonny caught four small rainbows and Earnest caught one large one.

"I only caught one," Earnest said.

The car continued to climb into the clouds. "I'm freezing," Earnest said. "This can't be June." Mr. Wheeler rolled up the windows and turned on the heater.

At a rest stop, Sonny and Earnest climbed a hill

to a patch of snow and had a fierce snowball fight. They sloshed back to the car soaking wet and red-faced, but full of laughter. Sonny put a snowball in the styrofoam cooler to take home.

"It's not as good as the snow back home," Earnest said. "It's too dry and powdery."

"Not as dry as your brain," Sonny snapped.

The car rolled on. Suddenly it was headed straight for a sheer mountain wall.

"Now what?" Earnest wanted to know. "Can we turn around and go back? This is a sign from God."

"Now we go *through* a mountain," Mr. Wheeler said. The car headed straight for a dark, black hole in the rock. "This is Eisenhower Tunnel," he explained. The car sped into the mouth of the tunnel, and Earnest curled up on the seat and put his hands over his head.

Sonny reached over the front seat and honked the horn three times and laughed at the echo. The tunnel was long and dimly lighted with eerie orange lights.

"Are we through it yet?" Earnest asked.

"Yep," Sonny replied, and Earnest looked up.

"We are not!" he yelled, and he buried his head back under his arms.

At last the sun again splashed on the car and Earnest came out of hiding.

"We just crossed the Continental Divide," Mrs. Wheeler said, pointing at a sign.

"What's that?" Sonny asked.

"It's the high spot of the country. From here all the water flows east behind us and west in front of us."

The car sped on past resorts and vacation villages. Strange-looking houses and hotels poked out from the aspen and pine trees.

"Ugly," Earnest said. "They look like big packing crates with windows."

Steel cables vined up the mountainsides. They were dotted with chairs for skiers to ride to the top.

"You wouldn't get me on one of those," Earnest announced. "You would have to be crazy to ride on one of those contraptions."

As evening shadows crept through the mountains, the boys sat back and relaxed. Slowly they realized the pine trees were thinning out and the mountains were changing from a steel-gray to a light brown color. The rocks were becoming more rugged and the slopes were strewn with big boulders.

The road narrowed to two lanes. "Going down," Mr. Wheeler said. "Down into Glenwood Canyon."

The boys sat up and stared out at the walls of the canyon. For the next half hour and car weaved back and forth through narrow rock passes. The road went down, down, down. The walls of the canyon were filled with dark caves and deep, mysterious gashes. Some of the rock formations hung way out over the road. It grew darker and darker as they went deeper and deeper into this great crack in the earth.

"I don't like this," Earnest said.

"Me neither," Sonny added.

Mrs. Wheeler shifted in her seat and clung to the door rest. "Ralph, it's time to find a motel. What are we gonna do?"

He pointed to the canyon wall. "We're going to stay in one of those caves."

"Not funny."

"We must be halfway to China," Sonny observed. "Look, Earnest's eyes were starting to slant already."

The car swayed back and forth around curves and nosed deeper and deeper into the mysterious rock grave. Just when it seemed they couldn't possibly go any deeper, the road leveled out. They rounded a bend and the setting sun shone on the beautiful valley town of Glenwood Springs.

"Here's where we spend the night," Mr. Wheeler said.

"Oh, it's beautiful!" Mrs. Wheeler said, with relief in her voice. "You really had me worried for a while, Ralph."

"Ah, civilization," Earnest said, with a sigh.

6 • Motel Extras

Mrs. Wheeler stretched in the motel doorway and breathed in the cool morning air. "Look at that, a snow-capped mountain put here just for us to see." Her voice was musical and her face glowed like the face of a little girl.

"Coming through," Sonny said, bumping the door with a suitcase.

In minutes they were back on the road. Behind them a bright sunrise played like a movie on the green-gray mountains. In front of them the mountains were smaller and treeless.

"These hills look like big sponges dipped in red ink," Earnest said. "Ugly, really ugly."

"I think they're neat," Sonny replied. He snapped pictures. Then he added, "Dad, I need to go to the rest room."

Mr. Wheeler looked at his wife and she looked back with a warning in her eyes. He braked hard and pulled to the edge of the road. Sonny leaped out, scrambled up a hill and disappeared behind a boulder.

"Hope a mountain lion gets him," Earnest mumbled.

Soon Sonny came bounding down the rocky hill with an armload of stones.

"Look at these beauties, Earnest," he said, laying the rocks on the back seat.

"Get rid of 'em," Mr. Wheeler warned. "I'm not carrying around a load of boulders, for crying out loud."

"Eeeeeww," Earnest said, as he fondled the stones. "Nasty."

"I'll put 'em in the trunk," Sonny promised. "Somewhere out of the way."

As the car droned on the air began to grow very warm. Little by little the earth grew flatter and drier and yellower. Small clumps of gray-green sagebrush were now the only living things to be seen.

Earnest perked up just in time to see the Utah state line sign. He grabbed his guidebook.

Sonny pointed to a tall tower-like rock jutting up from the desert floor. "What's that? It looks like a skyscraper without windows."

"That's a butt," Earnest said, glancing at his guidebook. "It says here we will see lots of butts in Utah."

Mrs. Wheeler looked at him strangely. "Butts? Oh, you mean *buttes*. Those are buttes, as in *beaut*iful. *Byoots*, not butts."

Earnest blushed. "Oh."

No other cars were on the road with them now. As far as they could see stretched the desert, strewn with boulders, pegged with buttes, and peppered with sagebrush.

Earnest rubbed his eyes. "My eyes are burning."

"Mine too," Sonny added. "And my nose is all dried out and my lips are getting chapped."

"It's the desert air," Mr. Wheeler explained. "And you better get used to it, 'cause we will be in it for a long, long time."

At last he pulled over for a rest. Mrs. Wheeler served everyone cups of water from the cooler.

Sonny wandered around the desert collecting sagebrush and other plants.

Earnest sat on a rock in the shade of the car. "Look at this forsaken place. It looks like something from Star Wars."

His mother sat down beside him. "Oh, I don't know. To me it's beautiful. It's just a different kind of beauty, that's all."

Sonny returned to the car with his pockets crammed with sagebrush. In his hands he was squeezing something.

"Look, Mom!" Peering from his hands was the pointed head of a lizard.

"Awwwkkk! Get that out of here, Sonny!"

Sonny opened his hands. The lizard leaped onto Earnest's arm, then sprang off to the desert floor and scampered away.

"See how they jump?" Sonny said. "Maybe that's why they call them leapin' lizards."

Sonny stuffed his sagebrush into the trunk. He thrust one piece in Earnest's face. "Here, smell this. It smells so good."

"Arrrrggghhhh," Earnest said, jerking away. "Putrid! Awful!"

Soon they were on their way again. The desert seemed endless. At last a very small village came into view on their right.

"Well," said Mr. Wheeler, "Here's where we camp for the night." Just before they turned off the exit, a signed loomed in front of them. *Next Service, 150 Miles,* it said.

Mrs. Wheeler gaped at the ramshackle town. "Ralph, you've got to be kidding. They don't have any motels in this place."

Earnest flipped through the guidebook. "They have one, but it's definitely not recommended."

Mr. Wheeler shrugged. "We have to take it," he

said. "The next town is a hundred fifty miles away, and it's smaller than this town."

"I just hope it has a pool," Sonny said.

"What a dreamer," Earnest replied. "We'll be lucky if it has drinking water."

The car rolled down a dusty street and turned in at the only motel sign. Mr. Wheeler twisted off the key and a tumbleweed bounced over the hood and rolled on by.

"Oh, Ralph, no! We can't stay here!"

The motel was a funeral parlor at one end, and a gas station at the other. Most of its grimy pink paint had been worn away by the desert sand. The doors were crooked and broken. Lying on the ground by the office sign was an old Indian lady, surrounded by the jewelry she was selling.

There was no pool, and only one other car.

Sonny was first to the room. He tugged on the screen door and it came off in his hand. He leaned it against the wall.

Inside, Sonny stopped and stared. "Look, the beds are sagging like a dinosaur slept in them."

The boys checked out the bathroom, which was no bigger than a closet. The drain was stopped up and the faucet dripped, causing the sink to overflow on the floor.

"There's your pool, Sonny," Earnest said, pointing to the puddle.

Mrs. Wheeler sniffed the air. "What's that horrible smell?" She rubbed the stained and torn carpet with her foot.

Mr. Wheeler just shrugged. "We can stand anything for one night. We're lucky to have a roof over our heads."

Mrs. Wheeler refused to undress for the night. "I'm not touching these sheets with my body. Let's just try to go to sleep and not think about it." Soon the family was settled in and the boys dozed off.

In the middle of the night the desert air turned cold. Mrs. Wheeler punched her husband. "Ralph, see if you can turn on some heat."

He clicked on a light and Mrs. Wheeler let out a scream. She jumped up and stomped toward the door. "I'm sleeping in the car!" she yelled, and the door slammed behind her.

Sonny and Earnest woke up. "What's her problem?" Earnest asked.

Mr. Wheeler pointed to the walls. Clinging to the grubby wallpaper were several small lizards and one big one. The boys grabbed their shoes and chased them, with little luck.

7 • A New Home

The Wheelers' car burst through the morning fog and started down into the San Bernardino Valley. The suffocating desert was behind them, and California looked like Heaven.

Even Earnest was interested in the strange new trees and plants that flew by the window.

"Look! Oranges. Everywhere!"

"Yeah, they look like orange bulbs hanging from round Christmas trees."

"What's that, in that field?"

"Grapes, those are grapes. Trillions of grapes."

"Oh, look at that funny tree."

"Whooo, it's shaped like Uncle Andy."

"What's that smell? Is there a perfume factory around here?"

"It's those hedges along the road. The flowers on them smell nice. Cherry would flip over all this stuff."

The hotel was easy to find, since it was the largest building in the area. Sonny gasped. "You mean we are staying *there?* It's humongous."

Mr. Wheeler turned into the entrance. Sonny leaped out and started to unload the trunk, but a bellboy beat him to it.

When they got inside, Sonny and Earnest just stood there staring with their mouths open.

"Does this make up for the motel in the desert?" Mr. Wheeler asked. "I've got to go register," he added. "I'll be right back."

Sonny spread his arms out. "This lobby is bigger than our gym at school."

"It's bigger than our whole *school*," Earnest corrected him.

Mrs. Wheeler and the boys sat by the large pool that filled the center of the lobby. They studied the fountains and strange sculptures that stuck up in the middle of the pool.

The boys took different elevators up to the fifth floor. Sonny was first at the door. He put the key card in the lock and waited for the green light to come on, then he shoved it open.

"What a room!" he shouted. "It even has a balcony with a picnic table. And look at that view!"

"Look at this," Earnest replied. "A TV that works, with remote and VCR, even."

When everyone was settled in, Mr. Wheeler explained the schedule. "I'll be in classes for the next two days, down on second floor. There's a swimming pool here on the fifth floor. Across the street is an amusement park. The beaches are just a nice walk down that way. There are gift shops and video games in the hotel. I'll join you at four each afternoon."

Earnest was trying hard not to look impressed, but a twinkle showed in his eyes.

Sonny and Earnest spent the rest of the day exploring the hundreds of rooms and halls of the hotel. They glided up and down escalators and raced the elevators to the top floor. They tromped up and down fire stairs and peered into dark rooms. Earnest made himself a map.

That evening the family ate in the hotel restaurant. Sonny was looking over his menu. "Hey, I

don't know what any of this stuff is. Doesn't any-
body around here speak English?"

"Look at these prices!" Earnest replied.
"There's nothing here less than twenty dollars."

Mr. Wheeler just smiled. "It's paid for. Eat
hearty."

The waitress was a Spanish girl with her black
hair in a bun. "Hello, my name is Rita, and I'll be
your waitress this evening."

Sonny turned to Earnest and mumbled, "Hello,
my name is Sonny, and I'll be your customer this
evening."

The next two days went too fast. The boys
swam in the pool until their skin was wrinkled.
They walked the beach, collecting shells and chasing gulls. With binoculars they followed the sail-
boats and big ships that crept by on the horizon.
They spent an afternoon at the amusement park
and played video games in the hotel. At one of the
gift shops Sonny spied a toy he wanted to buy.

"Look at that!" he said, pointing to a fish tank.
A little plastic, battery-powered frogman kept
swimming around and around in the tank.

"I want one of those," he said.

"You're crazy," Earnest warned. "It costs fifteen
bucks."

Back in the lobby, the boys sat by the fountain pool. Sonny put batteries in his frogman and tested its action. Then he lowered it into the pool.

"What are you doing?" Earnest yelled. "You saw the sign. Nothing goes in this pool or the security guards will nail you."

Too late. The toy was already kicking its way through the pool toward the restaurant.

"Sonny, you don't have all the dots on your dominos."

The plastic frogman at last bumped into the opposite wall of the pool, turned and headed back.

"Look," a man cried out. "Look at that!" He pointed to the frogman. Other businessmen and women gathered around to watch. Sonny beamed with pride, but Earnest grumbled. "Now you'll get caught for sure. I hope you spend the night in jail."

The little frogman suddenly turned and headed for a tall sculpture. Before Sonny could reach it, it paddled under the statue and stopped out of sight.

"I told you," Earnest said. "Now you're out fifteen bucks and tax."

Sonny just shrugged. "It was worth it," he said calmly.

Late that night Sonny was watching TV while his mother wrote postcards. Earnest and his father were already asleep. Sonny snapped off the TV and sat on the bed by his mother. "Mom, I've been thinking. I really feel bad about Cherry. That poor kid. She never gets to have fun."

"I know. It seems that way. But I wouldn't let it ruin your vacation. Cherry is a very smart girl. She'll be all right." She put away her pen. "By the way, is Earnest having any fun?"

Sonny shrugged. "Oh, sure. But he tries to act like he's bored, you know?"

Mrs. Wheeler winked. "He gets that from his dad."

Then she added, "Oh, say, speaking of Cherry, we got a postcard from her today." She pulled the wrinkled card from the phone drawer and shoved it at Sonny.

Sonny read the brief message on the card.

Dear Friends,
  I hope you all are having fun. Don't worry about me, I'm okay.

Cherish Elizabeth Pepper.
P.S. Hope Sonny wins the contest.

Sonny stared at the card. "It's a picture of the ocean. Wonder why she sent an ocean picture? I didn't know we had any oceans in Mulberry."

He smiled and handed the card back. Then he crawled under the sheets and sank his head into the pillow.

8 • Deep and Wide

The Wheelers gathered in the hotel lounge to wait for the bellboy to bring their baggage. They sat on the stone ledge around the fountain.

"Where's Earnest?" Mr. Wheeler asked.

Sonny shrugged. "Dunno. He was here a while ago. Maybe he's in the gift shop."

As the three of them waited, they studied the interesting people who walked back and forth in the lobby. People of every shape and every skin color. People who spoke different languages and dressed in all styles of clothes.

"Look at that man over there," Sonny said. "He looks just like Michael J. Fox. See?"

The man was sitting in a large soft chair near the restaurant entrance. He was reading a manuscript and playing with the knot of his tie. Sonny couldn't take his eyes off the man.

Sonny got up and wandered over closer for a better look. He leaned against a column and studied the small man.

A couple of girls blocked his view. They were whispering and giggling among themselves. All at once they walked right up to the man and said, "Are you Michael J. Fox?"

The man smiled at the girls and stood up. "In the flesh," he replied, pointing to himself with a smile. The girls gasped and stared at each other with wide eyes. Quickly they fished small tablets from their purses and thrust them at the man.

"Can we please have your autograph?"

Mr. Fox reached for the tablets and smiled. Sonny whirled around and raced back to his parents. "It's *him!*" he blurted out. He motioned for them to follow, but when the three of them arrived at the chair, the movie star was gone.

Just then Sonny spotted Earnest coming in the side entrance. In his arms he was carrying a large cardboard box, and two heavily loaded shopping bags hung from his arms.

"Earnest! Earnest! We just saw Michael J. Fox!"

Earnest plopped down the box and shopping bags and sat down to rest. "That's nice," he said calmly, his voice full of mockery. "And I was just having breakfast with the President of the United States when I got interrupted by the Queen of England," Earnest teased.

"No, really, I saw him, I saw him!"

Mrs. Wheeler peeked in the shopping bag. "Where have you been, Earnest? We almost left without you."

Earnest grinned a sheepish grin. "I found a library, just a block away. I saw it from our window with my binoculars. Look at all the good stuff I got." He opened the box, revealing a couple dozen old books. The shopping bags were full of the same.

"They were having a book sale, right out on the sidewalk. I got some beauties for only a dime each." His eyes seemed to shine.

Mr. Wheeler groaned. "Where on earth are we going to put them? The car is overloaded as it is."

"Don't worry," Earnest replied. "I've got it all figured out."

As the bellboy packed the trunk, Earnest stashed books in every nook and cranny in the car. Some he put under the front seats, some in the windows, and some in the door pockets. Last, he pulled up the back seat bottom and stuffed the rest of the books under it.

"Ready when you are," he called out.

Sonny wrinkled his nose. "Phew. Those old books stink."

"Not as bad as sagebrush," Earnest fired back.

"I really hate to leave that place," Sonny said, watching the hotel grow smaller through the rear window of the car.

"Well, I'm not sorry," Earnest replied. "Never seen so many strange people in all my life. When God made the world he must have tapped it on the end and let everything loose fall down into California."

"Where do we get on the freeway?" Mr. Wheeler asked Earnest.

Earnest squinted at his map. "In about two blocks."

"Uh-oh. We've got construction going on here. Hey, I can't get into the right lane because of all these machines."

"You've got to, Dad. Turn here, quick!"

"What? Where? Here?"

"No, wait, I mean . . ."

"Okay. *No! No!*"

"What are we doing?"

"This can't be right."

"Ralph, where are you going?"

"What's wrong?"

"Ralph, this is an exit ramp."

"Naw, you're crazy."

"I can't figure this out."

"Uh-oh, I think I goofed."

"Dad, I've got to go to the bathroom real bad . . ."

"Well, use your shoe!"

"Ralph, we're headed the wrong way! All the cars are coming at us!"

Earnest sat us and looked out the front window. "YO!" he yelled. He saw four lanes of cars coming at them. Headlights began to flash and horns honked as drivers circled wide around them.

"Ralph, we'll all be killed! Do something!"

Mr. Wheeler did something. He turned the car toward the grass. The car bounced up and over the curb and down the grassy embankment. It whumped and thumped through the ditch and up the other side.

"Ride 'em!" Sonny hollered. "Go, Dad, go!"

The car leaped and spun up the hill and staggered out onto a side street. He parked the car under a little shade tree and shut off the engine. He took a deep breath and said, "Let me see that map."

Sonny was grinning from ear to ear. He tapped Earnest on the shoulder. "You said it! You said it! You said the word!"

Earnest smacked his forehead. "I did? I did."

"You sure did. That's twice. One to go."

In a few minutes they were leaving Los Angeles. Then later, they left California itself. The air began to warm up as the desert returned, only now the desert was drier and whiter with odd-looking cactus trees.

"Ugly," Earnest said, over and over. "Really and truly ugly. This must be the armpit of the world."

"Do we go back through the mountains?" Sonny asked.

"Sure, but a different route. We'll see different things. Tomorrow we'll see the Grand Canyon."

Sonny perked up. "All right!"

It rained during the night. The motel near the canyon was nothing special, but it was dry and warm.

When Sonny opened the door next morning he let out a wail. "Fog! Look at it. I can't even see the office."

Mr. Wheeler looked out the window. "Hmmm. Not a good day for viewing the canyon, but maybe it will lift." For an hour they drove through fog so dense they couldn't read the road signs. The traffic began to pick up.

Suddenly a helicopter rumbled overhead, then another, and still another. "Either we're being invaded or we're near the canyon," Mr. Wheeler remarked. "Don't they give chopper rides over the canyon?"

At last the entrance to the canyon appeared through the fog. The road wound through fragrant pine trees and juniper bushes. Suddenly Sonny let out a cry. "Canyon ahead! The fog is clearing!" He stuck his body out the window and pointed at the great gorge in the earth. "Look at it. I can see for a hundred miles."

Mr. Wheeler parked near the rim. Everyone jumped out and ran to the edge to peer into the beautiful canyon.

Everyone except Earnest.

For a long time he just sat reading a magazine. He got out and sat on the rear bumper for

a while. Then slowly he ambled over to the others.
He glanced at the canyon, stretched, yawned, and
said, "When do we eat? I'm starved."

No one paid any attention to him. Mr. Wheeler
was busy explaining the wonders of the canyon.

"It's like an upside-down mountain. In some
places it's almost six thousand feet deep, as deep as
a mountain is high."

"How long is it, anyway?"

"Almost three hundred miles. It's hard to imag-
ine."

Sonny pranced around, snapping pictures cra-
zily. Other tourists crowded in around them.
Many of them were from other parts of the world.
Some spoke German, French, Italian, and other
languages. Two men wore robes and turbans.

"Gee," Sonny mumbled to himself. "Are we the
only Americans here? I thought this was *our*
canyon."

Earnest moseyed back to the car and curled up
with a book of word puzzles. Mrs. Wheeler noticed him leave. She slipped away from the crowd
and joined him in the back seat.

"Earnest?"

He went on reading, pretending not to hear her.

"Earnest, I know you don't like to travel, but I

feel like you are making yourself miserable for no reason."

Earnest put down the book and stared out the window into the trees.

"Earnest, what we appreciate in life, we get to keep. What we scorn, we lose."

Still he said nothing.

She went on. "I mean, what you look for in life is what you find. If you expect to be bored, you will be. If you look for good, you will find good. It's up to you."

Earnest still said nothing.

"Someday, Earnest, you will come back here to show this place to your children. I just hope they behave better than you."

She went back to the canyon edge.

Earnest pulled out his binoculars and studied the canyon from the car window. "Not a bad piece of work, God," he said quietly.

Far away some thunder rumbled long and low.

After lunch the car moaned on through the desert toward the mountains. The landscape began to take on bright and changing colors. A sign said, *You Are Entering the Painted Desert.*

"Whoever painted it," Earnest said, "needs a lesson in neatness."

No one paid any attention to him.

Far out in the desert the boys could see Indian sod huts. Around them stood old trucks and cars and gas tanks.

As the car started across a rock-strewn plain, signs appeared along the road. "Authentic Indian jewelry. Good prices."

"Stop, Dad!" Sonny sang out. "I want to get some jewelry for Cherry."

Mr. Wheeler slowed and spun in at the first booth, next to a teepee. Sonny leaped out and pored over the racks of sparkling jewelry. He couldn't seem to decide for a long time. At last he picked out a turquoise bracelet marked "$20." He handed it and his money to an Indian girl.

Earnest sneered at him. "Sonny, you sure don't know much about business. Never buy at the first place you come to. The prices are bound to get better farther on."

Sonny ignored him. As the car rolled on, more signs appeared along the road. "Indian Jewelry, 30% Off" and then "Jewelry, 60% Off."

"See," Earnest said. "I told you so." When the jewelry stands began to thin out, Earnest watched the signs closely. Then a sign said, "Last Chance for Indian Jewelry—Huge Discounts."

"Pull in here," Earnest shouted. Mr. Wheeler sighed, then pulled into the tourist parking place.

In moments Earnest was back in the car. He held up the same kind of bracelet Sonny had bought, only his had more stones in it. He smiled smugly and said, "Five dollars and fifty cents."

Sonny crossed his arms and said, "Who cares?"

9 • Downhill

Mrs. Wheeler was driving when the family got to the mountains again. Ralph Wheeler was asleep in the back seat with Earnest, and Sonny was riding in front.

The road was no longer a freeway but a narrow, two-lane road that wound back and forth, up and down. The edges of the road were crumbly, and Sonny kept glancing nervously over the ragged edges.

All at once smoke began to rise from under the hood. Mrs. Wheeler slowed the car. "Ralph!

Ralph! Wake up, we've got problems."

Mr. Wheeler jumped up and stared out the front window at the wisps of smoke rising from the edge of the hood. Then he sat back down. "It's nothing serious," he said. "Pull over at this little rest stop up here and I'll take care of it."

"Nothing serious? Since when is smoke nothing serious?" She angled off into a scenic rest stop by a mountain stream. The boys leaped out and began skipping rocks in the water.

Mr. Wheeler calmly lifted the hood of the car, humming happily to himself. "Joyce," he sang out, "get that big blanket out of the trunk and throw it over here and we'll have ourselves a picnic."

The boys gathered round their father to see what was going on. He just smiled. The smoke had died down. On top of the air cleaner the boys could see a large mound of aluminum foil. Carefully their father pried it loose and lifted off a square, flat box.

"What is it?" Sonny wanted to know.

"Smells like . . . like tomatoes," Earnest said.

Mr. Wheeler laid the box on the blanket and peeled away the foil.

"Pizza!" Sonny blurted out. "We're having hot pizza!"

Mrs. Wheeler shook her head. "What was it doing under the hood, Ralph?"

"I put it there. It's an old trick my father taught me. I bought this frozen pizza back at that mountain town, and the engine heat cooked it. It's a little crisp on the edges, but . . ."

"Amazing," Sonny said, over and over.

"Bet it tastes like motor oil," Earnest replied.

A family of chipmunks joined their pizza picnic, and the boys fed them bits of dough. It was hard to leave the beautiful view, but soon they rolled on through the mountains.

At Salida the boys collected rocks and minerals that sparkled in the soil along the road. They filled plastic bags with tiny slabs of clear mica, yellow chunks of fool's gold, and smooth, round pebbles of quartz. Now the trunk of the car was packed to the lid with every kind of plant and rock they had found. The strong odor of sagebrush tainted everything. Even their clothes smelled spicy and musty.

A little farther on they passed a small, worn sign that said *Ghost Town, Four Miles.* "Turn here!" Sonny shouted, and his father nearly drove off the road trying to turn. The gravel road wound around and around until they came to a deserted mining town. The boys wandered through the ruins while their parents caught a nap in the car.

"Didn't see a single lousy ghost," said Earnest, as they drove on down the mountain. The road seemed to go downhill forever, taking them to Canon City. On their left the Arkansas river snaked alongside them. Large orange rafts full of thrill-seekers bobbed and dipped along the rapids, and the boys begged for a raft ride, with no results.

Sonny was looking for toothpicks in the glove box when he noticed a little yellow button on the edge of the box frame.

"What's this button for?" He asked his father, as he stabbed it with his forefinger.

"DON'T TOUCH THAT BUTTON!" his father yelled too late. "That opens the trunk!"

Mr. Wheeler whirled around and saw sagebrush sailing through the air behind them, followed by plastic bags, wildflowers, and empty hamburger sacks. The trunk lid swayed up and down like a monster chewing on a salad.

Mr. Wheeler pulled over to repack the trunk. "Well, I don't think we lost anything important. Next time, Sonny, ask before you start pushing buttons."

Earnest sneered. "I'm sure glad to get rid of that stinkweed."

"Don't worry," Sonny replied. "There's more on the bottom."

The rest of the trip was routine. They stopped only for gas or motels. The boys played games in the back seat. Sonny tried every trick he knew to get Earnest to say the special word, but it was hopeless. The flat plains of Kansas did little to impress anyone.

On a Monday, two weeks from the day they left home, the scenery began to get familiar. The rolling fields of Missouri were covered as thick as fur with soybeans and corn. The air was heavy with humidity, and the western winds had slowed to a breeze.

When Sonny saw how near they were to home, he felt desperate. "I've got to get him to say 'Yo' one more time," he said to himself. He pulled a piece of paper and a pencil from the door pocket and scribbled something on the paper. Then he turned to Earnest.

"Earnest, here's a little quiz for you. You like word games."

Earnest perked up.

Sonny read the first question. "What goes up

and down on a string and spins round and round?"

Earnest started to answer, then checked himself. He just smiled.

"Okay, what do cowboys do when they sing?"

Still Earnest said nothing.

"All right, what do oxen wear when they are plowing a field?"

No response.

Sonny looked frustrated. "All right, one more. What is Mom's favorite milk dessert?"

Still Earnest just grinned. Then he said, "Sonny, give it up! You're so lame. You're just trying to get me to say that word I'm not gonna say. All those answers begin with the letters 'Y-O.' No way, O.J."

Sonny wadded up the paper and flung it on the floor. His face turned red and he leaped at Earnest like a wild man. He tried to strangle him, but he dropped to the floor giggling and shrieking.

"Say it!" Sonny screamed. "Say it, *say it*, SAY IT!" He pried at Earnest's lips with both hands. *"C'mon, say it or I'll beat you to a pulp!"*

Mr. Wheeler looked over the back seat and yelled, "Stop it! This is the very reason we came on this trip, to get over this kind of fighting. If I have to stop this car, the two of you can just walk the rest of the way home."

Earnest sat up and dusted himself off and tucked in his shirt. "Let's quit," he whispered to Sonny. "Before he gives us his famous 'wars' lecture."

By one in the afternoon the sign said, "Mulberry, Ten Miles." Earnest leaned over the front seat and stared out the front window for a glimpse of their town. At last the car began to slow down.

"We got a little rain while we were gone," Mr. Wheeler said, pointing at some puddles by the road. The car cruised on through town on Morley Highway.

Suddenly the tall, blue house loomed on the horizon. Earnest's eyes began to bulge as if they would pop out of his head. He took a deep breath, pointed at their house and shouted, "YO!" then, *"Land ho!"*

Sonny jumped up. "YOU SAID IT, YOU SAID IT! I WIN, I WIN!"

A look of horror came over Earnest. "Oops. What did I say?"

Sonny was laughing and clutching his stomach. "You said the magic word, that's what. I win, I win!"

10 • Shaving Cream

As soon as the car rolled to a standstill, Sonny sprang out and sprinted for the house.

"Where's he going in such a hurry?" Mrs. Wheeler asked.

"Where else?" Earnest muttered. "The rest room, of course."

After supper Cherry came by the house. She was smiling and her face was sunburned. More freckles than ever surrounded the tender eyes.

"Hi, Cherry!" Sonny said with a smile. Then he sobered his face and said, "I was worried about

you. I'm sorry we couldn't take you with us,
but . . ."

Cherry beamed. "That's okay. See, I went on a
trip too!"

"You did?"

"Yep. My grandma found me crying, so she
called the bus station and we took a bus trip to
New Orleans. Look, I brought you a souvenier."
She handed him a piece of driftwood. "It's from
the gulf."

Sonny winced. "You mean I worried about you
for nothing? See if I ever worry about you again."

Sonny brought out all the weeds and rocks he
had collected on the trip. For an hour the family
chattered and laughed over their good times.

Then Earnest left the room and came back with
the contract in his hand. "I have an announce-
ment to make," he said, clearing his throat. "Al-
though it pains me to say it, I did have a good time
on the trip . . ."

Sonny applauded and whistled, and his parents
joined him.

Earnest went on. "However, I did not have,
quote, 'more fun than I've ever had in my life.'"

"Uh-oh," Sonny said. He looked at his father
and his father was looking slightly pale.

"This means that one said father is required to eat one said mustache as per said contract spells out, which he may read if he wishes to refresh his memory." He handed the paper to his dad, then he handed him a small pair of scissors and electric razor.

Mr. Wheeler moaned. "How do I get in these messes?" He muttered to himself. "Oh, well, a promise is a promise."

"I've never seen Dad without his mustache," Sonny said with a laugh. "He's not really gonna eat it, is he? I don't believe it."

Mrs. Wheeler shrugged. "If he said he would, I guess he will."

Mr. Wheeler trudged to the bathroom, and the family waited outside the door.

Through the door they could hear snipping sounds, followed by the buzzing of the razor, and an occasional "ouch." Finally the door swung open and there stood Mr. Wheeler without his mustache.

"Oooog," Sonny said. "He looks naked. I can't stand it."

"*Eeeeyoo,*" Cherry added. "Put it back on, you look dorky."

Earnest smiled a broad smile. "YO!" he said.

Then he added, "Now, you got to eat 'em. That's the part I want to see."

In his hand Mr. Wheeler held a pile of whiskers. "Well, I guess I better get this overwith." He trudged to the kitchen and pulled a dish from the cupboard and filled it with ice cream from the refrigerator.

"You don't mind if I sweeten these hairs a little, do you?" he asked.

Earnest shrugged. "Suit yourself."

Mr. Wheeler sprinkled the whiskers on the ice cream and stirred them in good with his spoon. "This is what they call shaving cream."

"Ralph, you're not really going through with this, are you?"

"Why not? Whiskers are just good protein. No difference between this and a hamburger." He scooped up a big spoonful.

"Oh, I can't watch," Sonny groaned. "He's really gonna do it." He clutched his stomach and made gagging sounds.

"Me neither," Cherry said. She turned her head and giggled.

"I wouldn't miss it for the world," Earnest boasted.

Slowly Mr. Wheeler put a spoonful to his mouth and closed his lips over it. He slid the spoon out and began chewing.

"Ummmmm, not bad, not bad at all. 'Course, strawberry would be an improvement, but vanilla is not bad at all."

Cherry peeked, then Sonny.

"Arrrghhh, he did it!"

Mr. Wheeler continued to slurp and chew until all the ice cream and whiskers were gone. The family broke into cheers and applause, and he stood up to take a bow. He wiped a whisker from his lower lip and said, "The whole trip was worth it, just to enjoy this nice bowl of ice cream."

Earnest stuck out his hand. "Dad, I didn't think you would go through with it, but I guess I underestimated you." He shook his father's hand over and over.

Mr. Wheeler just smacked his lips.

Cherry and the boys went outside to check on things around the house.

Mr. Wheeler licked his spoon and said, "Do you have any more of those whiskers, Joyce?"

She got up and walked to the refrigerator. "I think so. And I think we've got some strawberry in here." She filled the dish with strawberry ice cream, then went to the cupboard. There she pulled out a small metal cheese grater and plopped it into a little yellow bowl. Last, she reached into a drawer and pulled out a big chocolate bar. Carefully she grated a big handful of chocolate "whiskers," which she sprinkled on the ice cream.

"Here, Ralph. Remember who saved your skin. You owe me one."

Mr. Wheeler raised the spoon to his mouth. "Don't worry, I won't forget." He licked his upper lip. "I just hope this mustache grows back soon."

Wheeler's Adventures

Wheeler's Big Break
Sonny and Earnest have a contest to see which one can fix the most broken items in one week.

Wheeler's Vacation
On a vacation to California, Earnest sets out to prove that he doesn't have to have fun if he doesn't want to.

Wheeler's Freedom
Sonny and Earnest are left home to take care of themselves for a whole week.

Wheeler's Campaign
The brothers agree to manage each other's campaigns for class president.